VANO AND NIKO

Copyright ©1986 Erlom Axvlediani / Siesta Publishing House.
Translation copyright ©2014 Mikheil Kakabadze
First edition, 2014 All rights reserved

Library of Congress Cataloging-in-Publication Data

Axvlediani, Erlom, 1933-2012.
  [Short stories. Selections. English]
  Vano and Niko / Erlom Akhvlediani ; translated from Georgian
  by Mikheil Kakabadze. -- First edition.
      pages cm
  ISBN 978-1-62897-106-4
  I. Kakabadze, Mikheil, translator.   II. Title.
PK9169.A924A2 2014
899'.969--dc23

                                    2014028690

Partially funded by a grant from the Illinois Arts Council, a state agency

This book is published with the support of the Georgian National Book Centre
and the Ministry of Culture and Monument Protection of Georgia

www.dalkeyarchive.com

Cover design and composition: Mikhail Iliatov
Printed on permanent / durable acid-free paper

ERLOM AKHVLEDIANI

VANO and NIKO

and

other stories

TRANSLATED BY MIKHEIL KAKABADZE

DALKEY ARCHIVE PRESS
Champaign / London / Dublin

TRANSLATOR'S PREFACE

IT WAS A HOT, DUSTY DAY IN TBILISI, Georgia, and my family and I had just met with Erlom and sat in a cool café. In the middle of a casual conversation, my father told Erlom the small news he wanted to share with him: I had just translated the first book of his trilogy, *Vano and Niko*, into English.

I was seventeen years old at that time. One year prior to our meeting with him, in the middle of translating a chapter of Camus's *La Peste* (my mother's "bizarre" way, it then seemed to me, to improve my French for school), my father interfered — with an idea that I'd be better off translating Erlom Akhvlediani's *Vano & Niko*.

A couple of years went by after I had translated *Vano & Niko*, and while negotiations about publishing were still ongoing, Erlom passed away. This was very sad news for everyone. My sorrow was made all the greater by the realisation that he wouldn't be around if my translation one day was accepted.

Recently, I was asked to translate the other two parts of the trilogy, *The Story of the Lazy Mouse* and *The Man Who Lost His Self and Other Stories*, and in the process of doing so, I retrospectively got to know the man Erlom was: a man filled with magic, mystery, and love, who wrote these beautiful little stories full of philosophical meaning and poetic insight.

It was precisely the subtleties of these messages and the meaning in the stories that was difficult to translate into English: a challenge typical when translating languages completely alien to each other. This isn't an excuse; it is well known that poetry and meaning always disappear to some extent in a translation. However, I would like to ask readers, once they come across what appears to them as something incomprehensible, to think in images instead of trying to dig too deep for the meaning, or not to try at all. Many of the stories are very poetic (particularly in *The Man Who Lost His Self and Other Stories*), and often the problems I faced while reading the stories over in English were the same ones I faced in my mother tongue.

I wish I had understood Erlom's wisdom many years ago. I surely would have avoided some mistakes and, at times, even pain. However, what I have gained by reading his stories again is invaluable, and for this I want to thank him with all my heart.

— Mikheil Kakabadze, 2014

VANO AND NIKO

1. ONCE

ONCE, VANO GOT UP LATER THAN USUAL, dressed quicker than usual, and ate breakfast faster than usual, so he'd get to work on time.

As soon as he went out, he met Niko.

"Hello!" said Niko.

"Hello!" answered Vano, and, with a quicker step than usual, he passed Niko so he could get to work on time.

When Vano was coming back home from work, he met Niko. They both remembered that in the morning they had greeted each other, so Niko gave Vano a smile. Vano returned the smile, and they both went on.

When Vano got home, he remembered that there was no bread in the cupboard. On his way to the bakery he met Niko. They both remembered that they had greeted each other in the morning, so Niko said hello to Vano again.

Vano said hello back, and they both went on their ways. When Vano was returning from the bakery, he met Niko. They both remembered that they had greeted each other in the morning, and Niko asked Vano:

"Are you taking home some bread?"

"Yes," Vano answered, and they both went on.

After Vano finished his meal, he remembered he had to get his tooth pulled out. As soon as he went out, he met Niko. They both remembered that they had greeted each other in the morning, so Niko avoided Vano's eye. Vano in turn avoided Niko's eye, and they both went on.

When Vano got his tooth pulled out and was angrily returning home, he met Niko. They both remembered that they had greeted each other in the morning, and Vano looked angrily at Niko. Niko returned the angry look, and they both went on.

When Vano got home, he remembered he had to go to the notary for some business. As soon as he went out, he met Niko. They both remembered that they had greeted each other in the morning, and Niko glared at Vano. Vano returned the glare, and they both went on.

When Vano arrived at the notary, he didn't get what he needed and he left for home, cursing. He met Niko on his way. They both remembered that they had greeted each other in the morning, and Vano slapped Niko. Niko returned the slap, and they both went on.

They both got home. They both had a drink. They both lay down on the couch, and they remembered that they had both greeted each other in the morning, so they both went out onto the street to meet each other.

Vano looked for Niko, and at last he found him. Niko looked for Vano, and at last he found him.

"Good night!" said Vano to Niko.

"Good night!" said Niko to Vano, and they both went on.

Vano and Niko didn't meet any more that day, but they each dreamed about the other during the night.

2. EVERYTHING WOULD BE ALL RIGHT

NIKO SOMETIMES TALKED ROUGHLY TO VANO.

Everything would (have been) be all right, if Niko (hadn't) didn't talk(ed) roughly to Vano, but everything wasn't all right, since Niko talked roughly to Vano.

Although Vano and Niko did not see each other very often, when they did see each other, Niko talked roughly to Vano.

This made Vano upset. He tried to keep up a good relationship with Niko, but Niko still talked roughly to Vano.

Vano had an old mother. Vano's mother was ill. Vano looked after his mother. The neighbors knew that Vano's mother was ill, and when Vano went to work, the yard-keeper lady used to ask him: "Vano, how is your mother?"

Vano would smile (first), say hello to the yard-keeper lady, and then he would sadly answer:

"She is ill. My mother's gotten old," and then he would become even sadder, since he would remember that Niko talked roughly to him.

When Vano would get home from work, he would push the chair next to his mother's bed. He would feed his ill mother, give her some water, stroke her head, and soothe her to sleep. He would sit there for hours and dream: "What would happen if Niko came and told me that, from this day on, he wouldn't talk roughly to me anymore? Then everything would be all right."

Time went by.

One day the yard-keeper lady told Vano she was sorry about his mother's death.

Vano smiled sadly at the yard-keeper lady and went on. Vano walked and thought: "She got old and died, poor mother ..." and then his face clouded over, as he remembered that Niko talked roughly to him.

There was a woman who worked with Vano. Vano liked this woman, and then he fell in love with her. The woman he fell in love with loved Vano too. Vano was happy but ... "I'll go and tell Niko not to talk to me roughly, and then everything will be all right ..." thought Vano, and walked on to meet the woman.

One day, Vano found out that the woman he loved had married another man. Vano's heart sank: "I guess she didn't love me. I guess she liked someone else ..." thought Vano—"... at least, from this day on, Niko shouldn't talk roughly to me."

But Niko talked roughly to Vano.

Everything would have been all right, if Niko hadn't talked roughly to Vano, but everything wasn't all right, since Niko talked roughly to Vano ...

3. VANO AND NIKO AND LAUGHING

ONCE NIKO SAT AND LAUGHED. Niko laughed and laughed.

Niko laughed on an empty stomach. Niko laughed at midday. And, in the evening, Niko laughed as well. Of course, at night, he nearly laughed his head off.

Vano stared at him and was surprised. Niko laughed.

Vano stared and wasn't surprised any more. Niko still laughed.

Vano looked around and thought to himself: "What is making Niko laugh?"

"Niko, this is a table."

Niko laughed.

Vano was happy it was the table that made Niko laugh, and he took the table outside.

Niko still laughed.

"Niko, this is a cupboard."

Niko laughed.

Vano was happy it was the cupboard that made Niko laugh, and he took the cupboard outside.

Niko still laughed.

"Niko, this is a bed."

Niko laughed.

Vano was happy it was the bed that made Niko laugh, and he took the bed outside.

Niko still laughed.

"Niko, this is an empty room," and Vano showed Niko the empty room.

Niko laughed.

Vano took the empty room outside.

Niko nearly laughed his head off.

Vano got angry. He rushed outside, fell on his knees and said:

"Niko, this is the sun—these are shadows."

Niko wanted to laugh.

"Niko, this is the evening—these are clouds."

Niko wanted to laugh.

"Niko! This is the sky—these are stars."

Niko wanted to laugh.

"Niko! This is sorrow—these are tears."

Niko wanted to laugh.

"This is life—and this is happiness, Niko!"

Niko wanted to laugh, but started to cry bitterly.

From that day on, Niko sometimes laughed and sometimes cried.

4. VANO AND NIKO AND MATCHES

VANO WAS STARING AT A WOMAN.

"Why are you staring at me? Do you like me?"

Vano was staring at the woman.

"Why are you staring at me? Don't you like me?"

Vano was staring at the woman.

"Why are you staring at me? Stop staring at me."

Vano wasn't staring at the woman anymore.

Vano took out a cigarette and then looked for some matches in his pockets for a long time.

"What are you looking for?"

Vano wasn't staring at the woman anymore. Vano was looking for matches.

"Matches? ... Here are some matches." And the woman picked up a dusty box of matches from the ground and gave it to Vano.

Vano smiled.

"Why are you smiling?"

Vano stopped smiling. Vano took the matches from her, took one matchstick out of the box and struck it against the box, but the wind blew the match out.

Vano put the burnt matchstick back into the box.

He struck the second match against the box, but that one, too, was blown out by the wind.

Vano put this burnt matchstick back into the box too.

He struck the third match against the box, and the wind didn't blow this one out. Vano lit his cigarette and handed the matches back to the woman.

"Remember this," the woman said, "Why are you staring at me? Have you fallen in love with me?"

Vano put the match box into the pocket next to his heart.

Vano and Niko were friends.

Vano loved Niko, just like Niko loved Vano. Vano also loved the woman whom he stared and stared at, and whom he fell in love with, and who gave him the matches as a keepsake ...

But one day Niko fell in love with the woman Vano loved ...

Vano and Niko were friends.

The next day, Niko went to Vano and asked him for a candle.

Vano only had one candle, but what could he do?—he took the candle and gave it to Niko ...

Thank God, Niko didn't ask him for matches ...

Niko went and lit the candle, and wrote a letter to the woman.

Vano and Niko were friends.

On the third day, Niko went to Vano and asked him for a hat.

Vano only had one hat, but what could he do?—he took the hat and gave it to Niko ...

Thank God Niko didn't ask him for matches ...

Niko went and put on the hat, and went on a date with the woman ...

Vano and Niko were friends.

Niko loved the woman very much, but he wished to love her even more. On the fourth day, Niko went over to Vano and asked him for love for the woman. Vano only had one love for the woman, but what could he do?—he took the love for the woman and gave it to Niko ...

Thank God Niko didn't ask for matches.

Niko went and fell in love with the woman even more.

Vano and Niko were friends.

When Niko fell in love with the woman even more, he wanted this love to last a long time, so on the fifth day, Niko went over to Vano and asked for his life. Vano only had one life, but what could he do?—he took the life and gave it to Niko ...

Thank God Niko didn't ask for matches.

Niko went, shared Vano's life with the woman, and they lived for a long time ...

Vano and Niko were friends ...

They were friends, Vano and Niko, and on the sixth day, Niko went over to Vano and asked his friend for loyalty. What could a friend do?—he took the loyalty and gave it to his friend ...

Thank God the friend didn't ask for matches ...

Vano didn't love the woman anymore, since he had no more love for the woman. Nor did the woman love Vano, since Vano didn't have the candle, or the hat, or the love for her, or life, or loyalty. That woman loved Niko ...

On the seventh day, Niko and Vano were standing on the street. Niko took out a cigarette and looked for some matches in his pockets for a long time.

"What are you looking for?" Vano asked.

Niko was looking for matches.

"You're not looking for matches, are you?" Vano asked with fear.

Niko was looking for matches.

Vano put his hand on the pocket by his heart and remembered:

"Why are you staring at me? Do you like me?"

"Why are you staring at me? Don't you like me?"

"Why are you staring at me ... Stop staring at me ..."

"What are you looking for?"

"Matches?—Here are some matches ..."

"Why are you smiling? ..."

"Take it as a keepsake."

Niko was looking for matches.

"Niko, I do have matches, but, please, don't ask me for them, or I'll give them to you ... It's a keepsake ..."

Niko went and asked somebody else for matches.

Niko and Vano were friends.

5. VANO AND NIKO AND THE DEBT

ONCE UPON A TIME, Vano was twenty years older than Niko ...

Niko owed Vano something, but Niko always cheated Vano. Today he would say, "Come tomorrow," the next day he would say, "Come tomorrow," and every day he would say, "Come tomorrow."

Vano was upset that Niko was cheating him and thought: "If he can pay me, he should pay me! If he cannot pay me, then why is he cheating me?! He should tell me directly and that's that."

But Niko didn't tell him directly, and if he said anything at all, he said: "Come tomorrow."

"If tomorrow he tells me again to come tomorrow, I'll give him an upset look. Then he'll finally understand that his cheating upsets me."

The next day Vano went to Niko.

"Hello!" said Niko.

"Hello!" answered Vano.

"What did you come for?" asked Niko.

"You owe me money," answered Vano.

"Come tomorrow," said Niko.

Vano got up, wasn't able to give Niko an upset look, and went off.

"I will go tomorrow again," thought Vano. "I'll go tomorrow again, and if tomorrow he tells me again to come tomorrow, then I will tell him he's cheating me. Then he'll understand that I know he's cheating me."

The next day Vano went to Niko.

"Hello!" said Niko.

"Hello!" answered Vano.

"What did you come for?" asked Niko.

"You owe me money," answered Vano.

"Come tomorrow," said Niko.

Vano got up and wasn't able to tell Niko, "Niko, I know you're cheating me," and went off.

"Niko is twenty years older than me," Vano thought. "If I were twenty years older than Niko, I would certainly pay the debt back to him. If he tells me again tomorrow that I should come tomorrow, then I will tell him he isn't a man of his word and it doesn't become one to behave like that. If only Niko were not twenty years older than me."

The next day Vano went to Niko.

"Hello!" said Niko.

"Hello!" answered Vano.

"What did you come for?" asked Niko.

"You owe me money," answered Vano.

"Come tomorrow," said Niko.

Vano got up and wasn't able to tell Niko, "Niko! You're not a man of your word, it's not appropriate to behave like that ... you are twenty years older than me," and went off.

"Ehh, if he tells me again tomorrow to come tomorrow," sighed Vano, "then I'll curse him out, I'll call him this and that ... Ehh, why am I not twenty years older than Niko?!"

The next day Vano went to Niko.

"Hello!" said Niko.

"Hello!" answered Vano.

"What did you come for?" asked Niko.

"You owe me money," answered Vano.

"Come tomorrow," said Niko.

Vano got up and wasn't able to tell Niko, "I should come tomorrow? If I were twenty years older than you … you this and that … huh!" and went off.

"I can't anymore," thought Vano. "I can't anymore. I'll go tomorrow again. I'll go tomorrow again and if he tells me again to come tomorrow, I'll have a stone in my pocket, and if he tells me to come tomorrow, I'll tell him I'll hit his head with the stone, and if he runs away, I will chase him … But I'll try not to catch up, I'll try not to hit him … "

The next day Vano went to Niko.

"Hello!" said Niko.

Vano didn't answer anything.

"What brought you here?"

"Your debt!"

"Tomorrow …"

Vano stood up and wasn't able to tell Niko, "Tomorrow?! … Run away! A stone is flying toward your head! Run! … I'll try not to catch up with you … I'll try not to hit you … Run! Fast!"

Niko didn't run away. Vano didn't run after him and didn't catch up with him. He didn't throw and didn't miss. He wasn't able to cry out to Niko, "I'm not going to come tomorrow, I'll come the day after tomorrow, and if you won't return your debt then I'll catch up with you. It's not for nothing that I'm twenty years younger than you," and he went off.

The next day Vano didn't go to Niko, but went looking for a big stone for him.

The third day Vano went to Niko.

"Hello!" said Niko.

"Hello!" answered Vano.

"What did you come for?" asked Niko.

"You owe me money," answered Vano.

"Tomorrow ..."

"What's that?!"

"Tomorrow ..."

"What's that?!"

"Don't come tomorrow, I'll give you your money today."

"Niko, I'm sorry I'm bothering you ... You are twenty years older than me ..."

Niko paid back the debt he owed to Vano.

6. STUPID VANO AND CLEVER NIKO

ONCE THEY SAID THIS: Vano is stupid, and Niko isn't stupid.

"What can I do? I'm stupid," thought Vano, and was still stupid.

"I'm clever!" Niko was happy.

"Ahh," sighed Niko to Vano, "what a misfortune, to be born only once and born stupid."

"Yes," Vano agreed, "to be born only once and born stupid, too. Well done to you, though, that you're not stupid but clever."

Vano was troubled that he was stupid.

Niko was happy, since he was clever.

Vano went out, and he was still stupid.

Niko did not go out, since he was clever.

Vano went out, always walking around, and was still stupid.

Niko did not go out, didn't walk around, since he was clever.

The sun was rising . . .

Vano was looking at how the sun was rising. He was saying "How nice!" and was still stupid.

Niko wasn't looking at how the sun was rising and wasn't saying anything, since he was clever.

. . . And the day came . . .

Vano was gazing at the day and was happy that it was day, and was still stupid.

Niko wasn't gazing at the day, since he was clever.

The sun was setting . . .

The sun was setting, and the west looked like a

purple dream. Vano was gazing at the sunset and was saying, "How nice!" and was still stupid.

Niko was clever.

Vano loved. Vano loved and cried. Vano cried and laughed. Vano laughed and was still stupid.

Niko wasn't stupid, since he did not love.

Life was nice, and Vano was saying, "How nice!" and Niko was clever.

"Ahh," sighed Niko to Vano, "what a misfortune, to be born only once and born stupid."

"Yes," Vano answered, "to be born only once and born stupid, too. Well done to you, though, that you're clever—how good!"

Days went by, and Vano was still stupid.

Days went by, since Niko was clever.

7. VANO AND NIKO AND HUNTING

ONCE NIKO THOUGHT THAT VANO WAS A BIRD, and he
himself was a hunter ...

Vano worried and thought: "What shall I do? I'm not
a bird, I'm Vano." But Niko didn't believe him. He
bought a double-barreled gun and started staring at the
sky. He was on the lookout, so that he could kill Vano
when he flew up. But the sky was empty.

Vano was afraid of actually turning into a bird and
flying up. He stuffed his pockets full of stones so he
wouldn't fly up; he avoided looking at the swallow so he
wouldn't learn to fly; he didn't stare at the sky so he
wouldn't want to fly up.

"Niko," Vano said to Niko, "throw away that gun
and stop staring at the sky. I'm not a bird, I'm Vano ..."

"You're a bird and that's it! You'll fly up and I'll shoot
you. I'm a hunter!"

"Niko," Vano said to Niko, "how can I be a bird
when I am Vano?"

"Stop arguing." Niko got angry. "Stop annoying me,
or I'll shoot you even if you're on the ground, as if
you've just landed."

Vano fell silent and walked away.

When he got home, Vano ate a big meal, attached a
few more pockets to his clothes, stuffed them full of
stones, and thought, "Perhaps Niko doesn't know what a
bird is; otherwise he wouldn't make a bird out of me. I'll
go and explain everything to him and then I won't need
to eat as much or have as many pockets."

Vano went over to Niko to explain to him what a
bird was.

"Niko," Vano began, "you don't know what a bird is."

"Of course I do!" Niko interrupted, "A bird has legs. You have legs too!"

"I have legs too …" Vano was worried.

"A bird has a body. You have a body too!"

"I have a body too …"

"A bird has eyes. You have eyes too!"

"I have eyes too …"

"So you're a bird, then!" Niko said triumphantly.

"Yes, but I have no wings, have I?"

Niko started to think. Niko started to think and then shouted at Vano angrily, "Quiet! You'll grow wings and will fly too … and if you won't grow any wings, be certain that I will kill you on the ground, like a wingless bird …"

Vano went home feeling worried. He was taking the stones out of his pockets and spreading them on the road like tears. And the tears were heavy as stones.

"What shall I do?" Vano thought while walking, spreading out the stones and crying. "What shall I do if I'm not a bird and can't fly? What shall I do if Niko is a hunter and wants to kill me? What shall I do if it makes no difference whether I fly up or not …"

The sun was setting …

Vano looked up the sky. Vano didn't have stones in his pockets anymore and felt much lighter. Vano looked at the swallow and learned to fly. Vano looked up the sky and wanted to fly …

"If I'm a bird, it's better to die up in the sky," he said and flew up.

The sky filled up. Niko aimed and shot. He shot and hit. He hit and dropped Vano.

"Weren't you saying you were not a bird?" Niko cried.

The sky turned empty again.

8. VANO AND NIKO AND TALL AND SHORT

1 cm

I

ONCE NIKO HAD NOTHING TO DO and said to Vano, "I am taller than you."

Vano got upset and answered, "And I am taller than you."

Niko got on his tiptoes and said to Vano, "Am I taller than you now?"

"Do you think I have no tiptoes?" Vano answered.

Niko jumped onto a chair and cried, "And now?"

Vano jumped up on a chair too.

Niko rushed outside, climbed up a tree, and cried to Vano: "Vano, look up!"

Vano didn't look up, climbed up another tree, and didn't say anything.

Niko jumped over to a mountain from the tree and cried from there to Vano,

"Hey, Vano, look how tall I am!"

Vano got on a mountain too, and cried to Niko,

"Hey, hey Niko!"

After that, Vano and Niko divided all the nearby mountains between them, piled them up on top of each other and got on top of them ... and one could hear them shouting,

"Hey, Vano, look at me! Look how tall I am!"

And from the ravines, cliffs, and abysses returned a thousand answers: "Hey Vano, look how taa-a-all I am!!!"

They got tired. Following narrow paths, they came back down. They put the mountains back where they belonged, brought out a level, evened out the ground, and compared heights.

They found out that each of them was taller than the other by a centimeter.

II

This time Vano had nothing to do and said to Niko:

"I am shorter than you."

Niko got upset and answered, "And I am shorter than you."

Vano fell on his knees and said to Niko, "Am I shorter than you now?"

Niko lay down on the floor: "And now?"

Vano dug out a bit of the ground and laid himself down: "Hey Niko, look how short I am!"

Niko dug out a bit of the ground too.

Vano dug out an entire hole.

Niko did the same.

Vano dug out a well.

Niko too.

They dug and dug, and one could hear voices: "Niko! Niko! Look down at how short I am …"

But Vano's voice was captured by the deep darkness, grew faint, and then, like a butterfly, died away.

They got tired. They climbed back up. They returned the earth back to the Earth, tamped it down, brought out a level, and compared heights.

They found out that each one of them was shorter than the other by a centimeter.

III

Once they both had something to do …

9. VANO AND NIKO ALMIGHTY

ONCE NIKO WAS ALMIGHTY. And Vano was Vano.

Almighty, as he was, Niko did what he wanted:

If he wanted to, he would chase a rabbit and if he wanted to, he would catch it too.

If he wanted to, he could bring down the sun and even store it in a chest.

If he wanted to, he wouldn't do anything and if he wanted to, he couldn't do anything.

In short, he did what he wanted to ... And then he would sit on a tall mountain and laugh.

I'm Niko almighty and
    I stayed up nights,
I'm Niko almighty and
    I turned black into white,
I'm Niko almighty and
    I turned even into odd,
I'm Niko almighty and
    I turned somebody else's into mine ...

Then he would laugh again:

It was ten, I made it a hundred,
    I'm Niko and I'm almighty,
It was a hundred—I made it one,
    I'm Niko and I'm almighty,
It was hideous, I made it the sun,
    I'm Niko and I'm almighty,
The sun was up, I brought it down,
    I'm Niko and I'm almighty.

Niko was laughing, the sun was hiding itself behind
the clouds, and the tree was running away. Birds
couldn't fly and the ants didn't even dare to crawl.
How could the moon rise? It couldn't, for fear.

At the very moment when Niko was sitting and
laughing on the tall mountain, Vano was standing on
a small mountain and thinking: "What am I able to
do?

"I can chase a rabbit, but can I catch it?

"I cannot reach the sun, and even if I do reach it,
can I bring it down?

"The only thing I can do is think, and even that I
cannot do that well."

Vano stood on a small mountain and worried.

"I'm Vano and that's it and I can only:

"let the night be a night,
    "let black stay black,
"let even stay even,
    "let somebody else's stay somebody else's."

Vano went on worrying.

"It is one and what can I change?!

"Let's say it became ten, still, what can I change?!

"It's hideous and all I can do is let it stay ugly …
Ehh!"

And from up above one could hear Niko's
uncontrollable laughter: "I'm Niko the almighty and
I'm Niko and I'm almighty …"

"Ehh," Vano sighed, "if only I were almighty like
Niko …" and Vano smiled. "Yes, if only I were
almighty like Niko, then …" and Vano sat up on the
small mountain and, smiling, he chanted:

"I would stay up the nights,
I would turn odds into evens,
I would turn ten into a hundred,
I would turn ugly into bright …
… and I would do everything right!"

Vano sang and sang, and in the end he decided to climb up the tall mountain and teach Niko this song.

But before he got to the top of the mountain, he forgot the lyrics to the song.

10. VANO AND SEVEN NIKOS

ONCE THERE WERE SEVEN NIKOS. There was only one
Vano, and he was little, too.

One of the Nikos raised Vano from a baby and
said, "Vano is mine."

The second Niko dressed Vano and said, "Vano is
mine."

The third Niko didn't raise Vano and didn't even
dress him but still said, "Vano is mine."

The fourth Niko put a hat on Vano. The hat was a
bit too big for Vano, since Vano was little, but the
fourth Niko still claimed that Vano belonged to him.

The fifth Niko was stronger than all the other
Nikos and said, "Vano is mine."

The sixth Niko didn't say anything, but this was
precisely to indicate that Vano was his.

The seventh Niko was Vano's teacher and taught
Vano a lot of things, but in the end he also wanted to
teach Vano that he belonged to him and nobody else.

Vano was little and there was only one of him, so
how could he know whose he was? Sometimes he said
to the first Niko, "I'm yours," sometimes he said to
the second Niko, "I'm yours." Sometimes he said to
the third Niko he was his, and sometimes he told all
of them together that he was theirs.

Once Vano went and sat under the big oak tree
and thought to himself, "Whose am I?

"I think I'm not the first Niko's. I think I'm not
the second Niko's either. To the third Niko, I belong
even less. To the fourth Niko? — No! To the fifth

Niko?—No! Nor do I belong to the seventh Niko, so how can I belong to the sixth Niko?"

Then he stood up, walked through a forest, and came out to a valley. He picked some flowers and looked up to the sky. Then he went back into the forest. He sat down under the oak tree again and suddenly said, "I think I am mine."

Vano got up and ran and was his own.

Vano got up and ran back and was his own.

Vano got up and cracked up laughing and was his own.

Vano fell down and started crying and was himself, his own.

It was painful, and Vano was his own.

He was singing, and Vano was his own.

He was happy, and Vano was his own.

Vano was dying, and he was himself, his own.

Vano was dying, little Vano, the one Vano, and he was happy that he was nobody's and was himself, his own ...

What a big flower the oak was.

11. LET IT BE YOURS

VANO AND NIKO WANDERED AROUND and loved this world. They climbed up the mountains' high peaks. From the peaks they came down to the valley, picked flowers, and the bright colors of the flowers made them happy. They went through forests that hadn't been walked through. They stared at the sun, and the sun high above made them happy. They sowed wheat. They reaped the wheat. They took it to the mill and there, the whole night, instead of tales, they told each other true stories . . .

Vano and Niko wandered around and this world made them happy.

Once the sun was setting.

"Niko," Vano said to Niko, "I'm sleepy, and I will go to sleep. When the sun rises, wake me up."

"Vano," Niko said to Vano, "I'm sleepy too, and I have to sleep too. And me? When the sun rises, who will wake me up?"

"Niko," said Vano, "then let's both go to sleep and the one who wakes up first, wakes the other one."

"Vano," said Niko, "let it be like this."

Both of them slept. The night, the enormous black light, flew over Niko and Vano and went off, far, far away.

The sun was rising . . .

Niko woke up.

"Vano, wake up." Niko started waking Vano up. "I already woke up."

Even though Vano really wanted to wake up, he couldn't.

So Niko shouted at Vano:

"Vano, here, I'm giving you a waking up, let it be yours!"

Vano woke up and the waking up was his.

"Oh, what a nice dream I had," Vano began. "Between the emerald mountains, a clean river flowed. The sun sat in that river. The water flowed over the sun. The sun cooled down and turned transparent. I looked into it and saw the sky. Golden fish swam in the sky. Then I looked closer and saw myself among them. I sat on a white horse and sang a song. Then I looked again, and far away, in the distance, on a pink cloud, I saw three women. When I came closer, there was just one woman sitting on the cloud, and even she was asleep ..."

"Oh, what a nice dream you've had, Vano," said Niko.

"Do you want it?!" exclaimed Vano.

"Yes I do!" Niko was happy.

"Here!" and Vano gave Niko his dream, and that wonderful dream, with those golden fish, that blue sky, that pink cloud, and that beautiful, sleeping woman, now belonged to Niko.

After this, it always happened like this:

... Spring would arrive. Under a bush a violet would open its eyes. Niko would squat in front of it. Then he would go over to Vano and say,

"Vano, look what a delicate violet I have."

Vano, even though he wanted it a lot, didn't have that flower.

"You want it?"

"Yes, I do," Vano would answer.

Then Niko would say to Vano:

"Let it be yours!"

Vano and Niko wandered around and Vano would see some nice stones. He would take them, toss them up and catch them, and then he would say to Niko,

"Do you want them to be yours?"

"Yes, I do," Niko would answer.

And a colorful stone was in his possession now.

Vano and Niko wandered around, and Niko would see a deer. He would see, chase, and catch it. Then he would go to Vano and say,

"Vano, do you want this deer?"

"Yes, I do," Vano would answer.

Then there was a beautiful field. Then a rustling forest. As the sun was setting, Vano said to Niko,

"Niko, look how wonderful the sunset is!"

And the sunset became Niko's.

But by the time the sun was rising, the sunrise already belonged to Vano.

Vano and Niko wandered around and hated this world, hated the mountains and the valleys, hated the rustling forest, hated the dreams and the deer, hated the sun and the colorful flowers ...

They sowed wheat, reaped the wheat, and when they got to the mill, they heaved sacks of grain at each other, and, in the end, tired and worn out, all day long, instead of telling each other the truth, they told each other tales ...

Vano and Niko wandered around ...

12. DON'T ASK FOR TOO MUCH, NIKO!

ONCE VANO WAS DAYDREAMING.

Niko was daydreaming too.

They both sat in a huge field with their backs against each other and stared into the distance.

"What if," mused Vano, "what if a person was born ..."

"And the sun rose in the east, and set in the west," mused Niko, "setting and single and clear."

"Don't ask for too much, Niko!"

Vano daydreamed.

Niko daydreamed too.

"What if the person grew," mused Vano, "grew and learned to stand ..."

" ... and the moon was in the sky, and stars," mused Niko, "if stars shone."

Vano mused:

"What if the person ran, jumped, chased butterflies and sometimes caught them, sometimes not ..."

Niko mused:

"And if in spring nature was happy and flowers bloomed; if in summer it was hot; if in autumn leaves fell off trees; if in winter it was cold, and snowed white snowflakes ... What if?!"

They both sat on the field, both looked into the distance, both daydreamed.

"What if the person sometimes got sick, sometimes was well? Sometimes wanting to sleep, sometimes sleeping. Sometimes dreaming. And if the

time came for him to fall in love with someone ...
and the time came for someone to love him?"

"And there would be this valley. This Vano, this
Niko, would both be staring into the distance. Both
musing ... What if?"

"Don't ask for too much, Niko!"

Vano daydreamed:

Niko daydreamed too.

"What if the the person had tears? If they felt like
crying, they cried; if they felt like laughing, they
laughed ..."

" ... and if there was earth ..."

"Don't ask for too much, Niko!"

Vano daydreamed:

"What if the person was dying?"

"Oh Vano, don't ask for too much!"

13. VANO IN NIKO'S DREAM

ONCE VANO WAS IN NIKO'S DREAM.

Niko would fall asleep, and a world would appear in his dream, where the sky was made of stone, the sun was made of wood, the wood was made of mist, the mist was made of earth, the earth was made of wind, the wind was made of lead; the lead, I don't remember what it was made of anymore …

Niko would sleep, and Vano would come into his dream …

Vano would come into Niko's dream and his thoughts would be made of ants, his dreams would be made of birds, his songs would be made of pebbles …

Vano would be walking in Niko's dream: he would walk through water and would catch fire; he would go up to the sun and would turn to ice; he would come here and would appear there; he would go there and would stay there; he would turn right and unfortunately not left.

Sometimes Vano would be in the night and sometimes the night would be in him.

Here he would see his worrying worries; there, tomorrow's grief would wait for him; and further away would be his loneliness.

Vano would sometimes be the branch of a tree — bending and suffering; sometimes he would be a leaf—turning yellow and falling to the ground. Down there would be the sky.

Niko would sleep, and a violet would be chasing a mosquito, the mosquito would be chasing a

grasshopper, the grasshopper a trout, the trout a
swallow, the swallow a shark, the shark a deer, the
deer a wolf, the wolf an eagle, the eagle a lion, the lion
a violet—the violet wouldn't run away, though, it
would just stay there ...

Vano would be walking around in Niko's dream
and yellow would be gray, gray would be orange,
orange would be green, green would be red, red would
be black, black would be turquoise, turquoise
wouldn't be anything ...

Vano would be walking around in Niko's dream
and wherever his shadow would fall, it would grow,
get a body, turn into an animal, and would crawl,
would rattle, and then disappear into the ground.

Niko would sleep and Vano would come into his
dream: sometimes happy and sometimes not;
sometimes merry and sometimes worried; sometimes
nice and sometimes mean.

Sometimes there would be one Vano, sometimes
there would be two Vanos, sometimes there would be
three Vanos, and sometimes there wouldn't even be
half a Vano.

There would be a lot of fruit in Niko's dream, but
every fruit would have the same taste.

Niko would sleep and the stone in his dream
would be full of worries, the stone would be full of
thoughts, the stone would be full of love, the stone
would be full of happiness, the stone would be full of
fear, the stone would be full of mistrust, the stone
would be full of loneliness, and the stone would be
empty of stone.

Vano would sometimes be born in Niko's dream,
would grow, turning into a man. Sometimes he would

shrink, empty out, and disappear.

Sometimes Vano would be a murderer, and sometimes he himself would be somewhere dead.

Niko would sleep and the seconds would be going around the oak; the days would be looking for their nights; the years would be on faraway roads; the centuries would lie on eternal fields, they would smoke pipes and talk.

Vano would be walking in Niko's dream, and when he woke up he would want to sleep, and when he was sleepy he would wake up.

Sometimes Vano would be in the rain, and sometimes the rain would be in him.

From time to time, Vano would have a dream of his own within Niko's dream. In Vano's dream a woman would come — his mother; and a man — his father; his sisters; his brothers; his dog; his wooden house; his small yard; his small garden …

In the morning the rooster would wake Niko up. Niko would get up and nothing that had been in his dream would be there.

Then night would come again, Niko would go to sleep, and Vano would come into his dream …

Once Vano went to the edge of Niko's dream and looked down. He looked down and saw: a field full of flowers, a forest full of trees, a day full of light. In the field was a beautiful woman. The woman was picking flowers and singing.

The rooster woke Niko up, the dream was gone, and of course, Vano too.

Night came and Niko would go to sleep again. Vano would come into his dream again.

Vano would walk through the water and would

catch fire; he would go up to the sun and would turn
to ice; he would turn right, unfortunately not left; he
would come here and would appear there; he would go
there and stay there. In the end he would still manage
to get to the edge of Niko's dream and would look
down: the sky would be made of sky, the soil of soil,
the night of night. He would also see a field full of
flowers. In the field would be a beautiful woman who
would be picking flowers and singing ...

Again and again, Niko would go to sleep. Again and
again, Vano would come into his dream. Again and
again, he would walk through water and catch fire ...
In the end Vano would still make it to the edge of
Niko's dream to see: stone made of stone, violets and
iris, rain made of rain, a beautiful woman who would
be picking flowers in fields and singing a song ...

Once Vano asked Niko to take him out of his
dream.

Niko took Vano out of his dream ...

On a sunny midday, on a dusty road, was seen, in
rags, a hungry and thirsty traveler, who was leaning on
a crutch and walking.

This traveler was Vano.

Vano stopped, wiped real sweat off his face, smiled,
and went on ...

14. BLUE-EYED VIOLET

ONCE THE MOST PRECIOUS WAS THE BLUE-EYED VIOLET ...

Niko shouted: "Blue-eyed violet! Blue-eyed violet!"

Vano was born.

Niko pleaded to the sky: "Blue-eyed violet! Blue-eyed violet! "

Vano grew up.

Niko still cried to the ground: "Blue-eyed violet! Blue-eyed violet!"

Vano turned into a man.

Niko still pleaded to the sky: "Blue-eyed violet! Blue-eyed violet!"

Vano married.

But Niko, again: "Blue-eyed and blue-eyed!"

Vano yoked the oxen.

But Niko, still: "Blue-eyed and blue-eyed!"

Vano worked the whole day.

And Niko: "Blue-eyed!"

Vano worked the next day as well.

Niko: "Blue-eyed!"

Vano worked the third day too.

And Niko ...

Vano named the first child Vano.

Niko ...

Vano named the second child Vano too.

And Niko ...

Vano sold crops in the town.

And Niko: "Blue-eyed!"

Vano named the third child Vano as well.

And Niko: "Blue-eyed and blue-eyed!"

Vano named the fourth child Niko.

And Niko cried: "Blue-eyed violet! Blue-eyed violet!"

Vano's last spring came. The snow melted. The ground peeked through. The air became a bit warmer. The sun shone a little bit brighter. One could see tiny buds on the branches.

Vano left the house.

Niko cried to the ground: "Blue-eyed violet! Blue-eyed violet!"

Vano came out of the house.

Niko pleaded with the sky: "Blue-eyed violet! Blue-eyed violet!"

Out came old Vano, who looked up at the sun, lit a pipe, and walked around the garden ...

By the fence grew a blue-eyed violet.

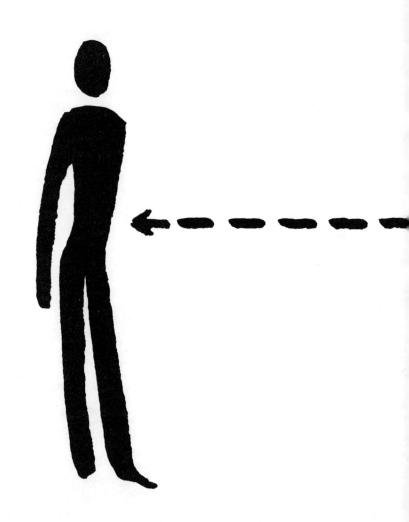

15. VANO AND NIKO AND NIKO AND VANO

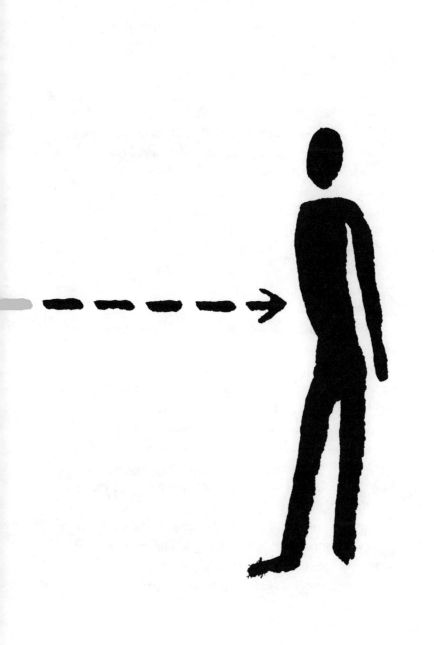

EARLIER ON, NIKO WAS VANO, VANO WAS NIKO.
Then Niko became Vano and Vano became Niko.
In the end, both became Vano.

And so it happened:

Niko was an evil person and did evil things to
others. Vano was a good person and always did good
things to others. But, just as people get bored of doing
the same thing all the time, Niko got bored of being
Niko, Vano got bored of being Vano.

Niko told Vano,

"Come on, let me be Vano!"

Vano was glad and answered,

"And I'll be Niko, all right?"

"As you like!"

And from that day on, Niko became Vano, Vano
became Niko.

It was a sunny day when Vano came out onto the
street. He ran here and rushed there. He saw a man
and laughed at him. He saw a woman and insulted
her. He saw a child and smacked its head. He saw a
dog and brandished his stick at it. He saw a robin and
threw a stone at it. He smashed all of the pots and
vases. He hit an axe against a tree. What else can I hit
it with? he wondered.

In short, Vano nikoed completely.

It was a sunny day, and Niko came out onto the
street too. He greeted people he knew nicely.
Sometimes he even greeted strangers. He patted the

children. He fed robins. What else can I feed them? he wondered. From time to time he even planted trees.

In short, Niko vanoed completely.

Time passed.

It was a cloudy day and vanoed Niko sat and was glad he had vanoed. He didn't even remember that he had once been Niko. Everyone loved him and he loved everyone. What more could he wish for?!

It was a cloudy day and nikoed Vano sat and remembered how he had once been Vano. He remembered how the man had been laughing. How the woman had been smiling. How the child had been growing. How the robin had been flying. How sweet the dog had been. How pretty the vases had looked. How the tree had been blossoming.

Then he remembered that he had nikoed and saw how the man had worried, how the woman had been upset, how the robin had been dying. How the vases had been smashed. How the tree had been moaning ...

He sighed,

"Ehh," and went to vanoed Niko and said, "You, vanoed Niko, I don't want to be Niko anymore, let me be Vano again."

"No," answered vanoed Niko.

"Please, let me be Vano again."

"No."

"Let me, or I'm nikoed now and I'll beat you, you hear me?"

Then vanoed Niko said,

"Let me stay Vano, please ... It's so good to be Vano, I want to stay Vano so much that ... Let me stay!"

Nikoed Vano frowned and answered, "I don't want

to be Niko anymore either ..."

Vanoed Niko became thoughtful, and then said, "You, nikoed Vano, I have an idea! Come on, you become Vano too and then we'll both be vanoed. Isn't it allowed to have two Vanos?"

Nikoed Vano tried hard, and finally vanoed again, even though it was a rainy day.

That is how Vano nikoed and Niko vanoed. In the end, though, they both vanoed.

AND OTHER STORIES

THE STORY OF A LAZY MOUSE

1. THE FOX AND THE LIE

There was a time when things which are now invisible, were visible. Truth and untruth, good and evil, loyalty and disloyalty were seen as clearly as squirrels and goats, camels and cloves, fish and nightingales. If you went left you would spot the flower of truth, pluck it and tie it to your heart so that you and everyone else would see what a truthful person you were. If you went right you would see the lie trying to climb down the rabbit hole. If you wished, you would catch the lie and put it in your coat pocket. The lie in your pocket would then make you lie in such a way that you surprised even yourself.

In those times there was no one as honest or as kind as the fox. The fox gained such a reputation for his honesty (he didn't even need to wear the flowers of truth) that all the animals of the forest, the birds in the sky, and even us human beings would say things like, "That bear is so fox-like," or, "He's so fox-like," instead of, "Isn't he so honest?"

When the fox went for a walk, the animals of the forest and the birds of the sky would gather around him and ask him all kinds of questions. The bear would ask: "Which is truer: that the poppy is a poppy or that I'm a bear?" And the fox would respond: "The truth is that you are a bear, but the poppy is more of a poppy."

The pig would ask: "What is it that forces the rain

to fall?" And the fox would answer: "It rains because even the smoggy air wants to wash its body!" And the pig would walk away, blushing, since it was dirty and covered in mud.

One time, night fell. The forest was sleeping deeply. So deeply that even the most cunning lie would find it difficult to enter. However, the lie still managed to slip into the forest. The wolf and the lion, the rabbit and the mouse, the oak and the crow, the violets and the fawn were all forced to dream lying dreams. The lion dreamt that the rabbit was hunting him. The poor lion was covered in cold sweat. The rose dreamt that the black raven was sitting on him instead of the nightingale and was screaming in vain. The mouse dreamt that he was a cat and was chasing his brother mice around. The forest itself dreamt that it was a desert, thirsty and soulless.

The sun rose. The forest awoke from its deep sleep. Everyone opened their eyes and immediately spotted the lie. The lie that made them all dream such dreams. The whole forest started hunting the lie. Meanwhile, the fox was walking along the path of truth. He was on his way to the garden of truth to water the flowers of truth. Suddenly, the lie appeared in front of him.

"Where to, lie?" asked the fox.

"I'm on my way to the garden of truth," lied the lie. "I have to wash away my sins."

"I'm also on the way to the garden of truth, let's go together!" said the fox.

"No one will let me in the garden. Unless you hide me somewhere!" suggested the lie.

"But I can't hide you anywhere, I don't have any clothes on," replied the fox.

"I can hide in you! Once we get to the garden you can let me out," said the lie.

"Alright, hide in me," said the fox and opened his mouth wide.

The lie jumped, giggling, into the fox's mouth, ran down his throat, and through his heart, and settled in his tail. At the same moment all the forest's animals and the birds of the sky burst out of the forest. They surrounded the fox and asked him: "Dear fox, did you by any chance come across the lie? He made all of us dream lying dreams, and now we have to get rid of him once and for all."

The fox wanted to tell them the truth, but the cunning lie in his tail made him say, "He went that way," and point out the direction. All the animals, trusting the fox, went where he told them to go.

That is how the lie made the fox lie. That is how the fox's reputation as the most honest animal was damaged.

The fox wants to be honest, but he can't anymore. From time to time he remembers that he was once an honest being (once the lie inside his tail falls asleep), and how everybody loved him, and how all the animals of the forest and all the birds of the sky trusted him. He wonders maybe if he were to sneeze, he could get rid of the lie once and for all, but the lie is sitting comfortably in a nice, warm spot in the fox's tail and has no plans to come out. The lie thinks to himself: "They're blaming the fox for all the lies and I don't think I'll ever find a better spot than this."

2. THE WHITE FLOWER AND THE WHITE BUTTERFLY

Near a fence, a beautiful white flower blossomed on a tall stem. The white butterfly spotted the white flower right away and flew towards it. She circled the flower a couple of times and landed on the fence.

"Let's fly away together!" suggested the butterfly to the flower.

"I don't know how to fly," answered the flower.

"You don't know how to fly? But we look so alike," said the butterfly.

"Yes, we look alike, but I somehow can't manage to fly ..." replied the flower.

"That's impossible! You're mistaken. Come now, we'll fly right away!"

"But I've really never flown!"

"Are you saying that you've never moved from your spot?"

"Yes ..."

"Have you never visited anyone?"

"Never. I'm tied to the ground by the stem."

"You're talking nonsense. What do you need that stem for anyway? Just try to fly upwards and you'll realize how easy it is!"

"I'm not allowed to ..."

"Trust me, we'll fly away together, and I'll take you to a beautiful field I know!"

"Can you fly to that beautiful field and then fly back again and describe it to me?"

"No, no. You just try flying upwards and you'll realize how easy it is."

The white flower tried flying up, broke off its stem

and fell down right away. The butterfly circled the
flower a couple of times.

"You truly don't know how to fly …" she thought
to herself, flew over the fence and out of sight.

3. THE UNTALENTED SPIDER

In a small hole between bricks there lived mother
spider and father spider. They had three children and
they were three little spiders. Once the three spiders
were old enough, the parents brought them to the
famous weaver spider to learn the craft of spinning. Is
a spider a spider if he doesn't know how to spin a web?

The weaver spider lived in a large cellar. In all the
corners, and on the walls and the ceiling of the cellar
there were webs spun by the spider and his
apprentices.

Two of the young spiders learnt quickly. The third
spider, however, was untalented, and no matter how
hard he tried, he couldn't learn the skill of spinning.
In the end he got bored and started walking around
the cellar.

Suddenly, he heard a buzzing. As he came closer,
he saw that there was a fly stuck in a web. He was
surprised and asked the fly how he was making that
buzzing sound. The fly found the spider's question
even more surprising and stopped buzzing right away.

"Set me free," he said, "and I'll teach you how to
buzz."

The spider set him free instantly, and the fly kept
his word—he taught the spider how to buzz. That

same day, wherever the spider saw a web, he would climb into it and start buzzing. Large spiders would run out from every side and couldn't believe their eyes when they saw that, instead of their prey, there was a small spider sitting in the middle of the web. The large spiders would then return, disappointed, back to their homes.

4. THE STORY OF THE LAZY MOUSE

It was dawn. The mouse woke up, stretched and thought to himself: "I will get up, wash myself, breakfast, and get myself ready for hunting." He rolled over onto his second side and continued thinking, "I will get ready for hunting, poke my head out of the hole, and look to the right and to the left." He rolled over onto his third side and further thought: "I will look around, then I will get out of the hole, and advance fearlessly towards the cellar." The mouse rolled over onto his fourth side and thought: "I will enter the cellar and spot the mousetrap ..." and again he rolled over, onto his fifth side.

This time the mouse was occupied with the mousetrap. While the mouse is thinking, let us also think for a moment and ask ourselves: "Why does the mouse have so many sides?"

The reason is that he is lazy. The lazier a mouse is, or a cat, or a dog, the more sides he has, so that he can keep on turning in his bed, from one side to the other. There is an example of a certain lazy boy who has so many sides that he has been counting them for over a hundred years, and has still not reached the end.

On which side should we stop with the mouse? On the fifth? All right.

The mouse rolled over onto his fifth side and continued thinking: "I will spot the mousetrap and tip-toe around it so silently that it won't hear me. Once he hears me it will be too late, and he will get very angry. By the time he gets angry, I'll already be far away, so the mousetrap won't have anyone to catch. Since he won't have anyone to capture, he will capture himself."

The mouse got so carried away by his thoughts that he rolled over right onto his seventh side, skipping the sixth. "As soon as the trap captures itself, the noise will wake up the cat," he thought to himself. Thinking about the cat frightened him so much that he quickly turned back onto his fifth side, again skipping the sixth. It took him a while to calm down, and once he did he rolled over onto his sixth side. "The cat won't wake up. Cats usually prefer sleeping than waking up! If he wakes up, he won't be able to dream anymore!"

The mouse continued wondering and rolled over onto his eighth side. "The cat won't wake up, and in the dark corner of the cellar I will spot the piece of dried, white cheese that my brave neighbor, Little Mouse, saw the other day."

The mouse rolled over onto his ninth side and continued wondering: "I will spot the dry piece of white cheese and slowly approach it. They say that the piece of cheese gets bigger the closer you are to it!"

The mouse rolled over onto his tenth side and thought: "If a piece of dry cheese lay there yesterday then, obviously, it will be there today, which means that it will also be there tomorrow!" The mouse rolled over onto his eleventh side and fell asleep.

It was so dark when the mouse woke up that he thought it had to be night and went back to sleep. He woke up again but it wasn't dawn yet—so he went back to sleep. He woke up once again but it was dark again. "I must have missed the day," he thought to himself and went back to sleep.

The mouse later realized that the night couldn't be this dark but that someone had filled in his hole. Right now I don't even know if the mouse is sleeping or not. I think he doesn't know either if he's sleeping or not, since it is so dark down there.

5. THE TEACHER FOX

Once a light-headed and idle hen gave her seven chicks to the fox to bring up. The fox had wanted to do so from the start. He took the chicks to his burrow and started to bring them up.

He taught the first chick to count to six.

The second chick, to five.

The third chick, to four.

The fourth chick, to three.

The fifth chick, to two.

The sixth chick, to one.

The seventh chick was taught nothing.

Time passed.

For the first chick only six days passed. For the second, five. He only knew how to count to five. The third chick counted and counted, and managed to count to four. "Only four days must have passed," he thought. For the fourth chick, only three days passed. The fifth chick saw the big sun rise only twice. The sixth chick, once.

For the seventh chick not even one day passed, it was all the same day. The seventh chick didn't know how to count, so how could he have counted the days?

The fox got hungry. He gathered the seven chicks together and put on his glasses. The teacher fox was preparing an exam for the chicks. Of course, he could have just swallowed all seven of them without testing them first, but he didn't want to appear unjust.

The fox wrote the task on the board: Chicks, your mother brought you to me to bring you up. During the springtime there were seven of you. During the whole summer, I was taking care of you. I was feeding you, clothing you, not letting the cold breeze get to you, guarding you, not letting the jackal capture you, not letting the falcon snatch you. I was also holding myself back, not swallowing someone disobedient or pushy. And what do you see? All of you are still here!

The question is the following: How many of you were left during the springtime?

"Six!" answered the first chick, which only knew how to count to six.

The fox swallowed the first chick for giving the wrong answer.

"And now?" the fox asked the second chick.

"Five!" said the second chick.

"Wrong answer!" said the fox and swallowed him.

"Four," said the third. The fox swallowed him.

"Three," said the fourth chick, not thinking. He too was swallowed.

The fifth chick also answered falsely and was eaten.

"There's only one left!" cried the sixth. He sensed that he too would be eaten, and so it happened.

Now there was only the seventh chick left. He was sitting happily in a corner of the burrow.

"How many of you are left?" the fox asked the last chick.

"None," the last chick replied, since he didn't know how to count.

The fox wanted to eat him as well, but since there were "none" left, what would he eat?

Instead, the last chick ate the fox, since he had been left uneducated and didn't even know that chicks don't eat fox!

THE MAN WHO LOST HIS SELF
& OTHER STORIES

1. THE STORY OF AN INVENTOR MAN

Once there was an inventor man. He invented everything. He invented things that hadn't been invented yet, and he also invented things that had already been invented. He invented things that aren't worth inventing and he invented things that are impossible to invent.

Once there was a perfect man, an inventor man. First, he invented himself. He then invented a mountain, and at the foot of the mountain he invented a hut. After that, he invented peaceful life and went to live in the hut he had invented.

The others heard of the inventor man. They visited him and asked him to invent them as well, and so the inventor man invented us. Finally, he invented an infinite road and went on to take that road.

2. THE STORY OF A MAN

Once there was a man who had his own worries. "Why am I only one?" he asked himself. Sometimes he went this way—since he was only one—sometimes the other.

The others used to calm him down: "You have nothing to worry about. Aren't we all single people?"

"No," he would answer. "There are so many people

in this world. Is there no one else who is me as well?!"

He went on his way. "Maybe I'll find another me," he thought.

He wondered to himself, "One me could look at the sky while the other me could stare at the ground! One me could sing while the other me could dance! While one me would hurt, the other me would just be. While one me would die, the other me would live on ..."

He got tired and fell asleep.

While sleeping, he dreamt that everyone else was him.

He woke up frightened and quickly returned to his village.

3. THE STORY OF AN UNHAPPY MAN

There was once an unhappy man. He was unhappier than the unhappy, and even unhappier than that.

His close relatives paid him a visit and asked him how he was.

"How do you think?" the unhappy man answered. "I have a chicken. I wake up in the morning, thinking that I woke up by myself, only to realize that the chicken woke me up! I get up and slaughter it. I get dinner ready, eat, and go to sleep. I wake up, thinking that I woke up by myself, again to realize that the chicken woke me up! I get up and slaughter it, get dinner ready, eat it. I'm fed up eating chicken meat the whole time!"

"You truly are an unhappy man," his relatives said reassuringly.

Now his acquaintances arrived. They asked him how he was.

"How do you think?" sighed the unhappy man. "I have a goat. It won't stop bothering me. Every morning I sell it, and every evening it's returned to me. You see it? It's being returned to me right this moment! I just can't get rid of it."

"You truly are an unhappy man," his acquaintances said, and left.

Now completely foreign people arrived. They had heard of the man's unhappy state.

"How are you?" they asked.

"Oh!" the unhappy man waved his hand dismissingly. "I have a wife. She loves me, and I love her too, but I'm a man, and no man has built a life based only on love. So I take her to the water and throw her into it. I wake up in the morning and what do my eyes see? My wife lying next to me, loving me more than ever, and I'm loving her more than ever as well. Everyday I'm suffering this way and then all these people are visiting me and asking me how I am, annoying me and reminding me of my terrible state ..."

4. THE STORY OF A LONELY MAN

Once there was a lonely man. One day a chicken came to the man's house. The man's neighbor asked him, "How is your chicken?"

"He's very good! He wakes me up in the morning so I'm never late to work."

Another neighbor asked him, "How is your chicken doing?"

"There's no other chicken like this one," he answered. "When I return home in the evenings he has tasty dishes ready for me."

"How is your chicken?" they asked.

"He plays the chonguri-guitar and sings along sweetly."

"Come on, tell us more about your chicken!"

"He's a friend, a true friend. Just recently my chicken saved me from a pack of wolves."

The neighbors couldn't get enough and asked again how the chicken was.

"How is he?" he said. "Recently the chicken and I drank together. We had a lot of wine but didn't have much to eat. We got into a little row. A fight started between us and we reached for knives. What happened afterwards I don't remember so well. I woke up in the morning and what did I see? — a pair of chicken bones on my plate."

The man was left lonely once again.

5. THE STORY OF A FORGETFUL MAN

Once there was a forgetful man. He forgot everything. First he forgot his dream. Then he forgot to wash his face. He couldn't remember if he had breakfasted anymore, and just in case he hadn't, he breakfasted a couple of times. He then forgot to go to work, so he stayed at home. He also forgot that he had stayed home, so he stayed home again.

The forgetful man forgot that he had a wife, so he married another woman and forgot to let go of his first wife. He also forgot to let go of his second wife and married a third woman.

The forgetful man only remembered once that he was forgetful, and remembered all the debts he had. The forgetful man felt guilty. He had been trying to remember his forgetfulness for a long time and at last he remembered. He forgot even more than he knew. In the end, the forgetful man had nothing more to forget and forgot about life.

6. THE STORY OF A KIND MAN

Once there was a kind man. His wife was also kind and so were their children. He also had a donkey. The donkey would also have been kind, if it hadn't been born a donkey.

Once the kind man had to travel from one village to another. He climbed on his donkey and got on his way. After travelling a short distance he came across an elderly person. The kind man was kind, so he lifted the elderly person up onto his donkey.

He travelled another short distance and came across a child. The kind man was kind, so he lifted the child onto his donkey.

He travelled another short distance and came across two women; one was pretty and the other was not pretty. He lifted them both onto his donkey.

He travelled another short distance and spotted a camel that had fallen over, with baggage lying next to it. The owner sat beside the camel, crying. The kind man was kind so he lifted the camel with the baggage and the man with his tears up onto the donkey.

He travelled another short distance and saw a boulder lying by the road. The kind man was kind, so he lifted the boulder up onto the donkey.

He travelled another short distance and the donkey said to the kind man, "Kind man, please lift me up onto a donkey as well."

The kind man was kind, so he lifted the donkey with his load up onto another donkey.

They travelled another short distance and arrived at the village.

7. THE STORY OF A CAUTIOUS MAN

Once there was a cautious man. He was so cautious that he was afraid to leave his home. He said to himself, "What if, when I leave my home, I come across someone ill-tempered? What if he wants to fight me and beats me up? No, I won't leave my home!"

He said to himself, "What if when I leave my home I meet a woman I like, and she starts liking me too? What if I fall in love with her, and she falls in love with me too? What if I ask her to marry me, and she says she wants to marry me too? No, I won't leave my home!"

He said to himself, "What if when I leave my home, my wife finds a lover? What if they start having an affair, and I don't know about it? No, I won't leave my home!"

He said to himself, "What if, when I leave my home, my child strikes a match? What if the house catches fire, and my child suffocates in the house? No, I won't leave my house!"

He said to himself, "What if the ceiling collapses, if I stay home, and I end up underneath it?"

8. THE STORY OF A STINGY MAN

Once there was a man who possessed a lot of money. He didn't want to spend it, and his money got tired of being a do-nothing and squandered the penny-pincher himself. First he lavishly spent the man's honesty, together with large sums of money on a feast. What was left from the feast he divided between the middle sums of money. The leftovers were given to the change.

He blew the man's loyalty on his hangover.

He lost his love on a gamble.

He pawned his bravery.

Sympathy, soft-heartedness, and tenderness were thrown away with the dice.

Generosity and patience were given away as a bribe.

The rest of his small talents were tossed to bum and fake moneys.

In the end, what remained from the man was a check.

With the worn-out check he hoped to redeem any of the man's skills, but it too was blown away by the wind and was lost.

And the man was left alone, homeless, shattered, and stuffed-sewn-forgotten in a pillow.

9. THE STORY OF THE HALF MAN

Once there was a half man. The half man's wife was also half, and so were his children. The half man lived in a half way. His joy was half, and so was his sorrow.

Once the half man woke up and realized he was whole. Everything around him turned whole—the sun, the moon, the stars. The half man's wife and children became whole as well. The half man's sorrow also became whole. He didn't know what to do anymore about his wholeness.

Earlier, in the good old days, everything was half-half and so were his duties and responsibilities.

Now he had to get work done. He had to feel pain in its fullness. Joy and sorrow had to be felt in their wholeness. He had to open his heart fully to others.

Lost in these thoughts, the half man fell into a deep sleep. When he woke up, he realized, to his delight, that not only was he not whole, but he wasn't half anymore either.

The half man had become a quarter man.

10. THE STORY OF A MAN WHO LOVED HIS COUNTRY

Once there was a man who loved his country.

"Tell us how much you love your country," they said to him.

"Very much. There's nothing I wouldn't do for my country," he answered.

"Imagine your neighbor doesn't love your country as much as you do. What would you do?" they asked.

"I would chop him up into bits and toss the pieces to the crows to eat," he answered.

"What would you do with his beautiful wife?" they asked.

"I will make her my property," he answered.

"What will you do to his small child?" they asked.

"I will sell him to Istanbul as a slave," he answered.

"What will you do to his house and garden, to his meadows and cattle, and everything that had belonged to him?" they asked.

"I will share the belongings with those who love my country as I do," he answered.

11. THE STORY OF AN ENVIOUS MAN

Once there was an envious man. He was envious of everything and everybody. If he was home his envy suffocated him. If he left his home his envy blinded him and darkened his path.

When he woke up he was envious of going to bed. When he opened his eyes he was envious of closing his eyes. When he looked to the right he was envious of looking to the left. The envious man hated and was envious of loving. The envious man loved and was envious of hating.

The envious man was possessed by envy …

Once he decided to take revenge on envy.

First he envied fish and he learnt to swim.

He envied birds and learnt to fly.

He envied the dogs' loyalty and became as loyal as a dog.

He envied the sheep's braininess and became as brainy as the sheep.

Finally, he envied the tree that it stood there on the same spot, throwing a cooling shadow, and had fruits, and had leaves that rustled, and had birds resting on its branches, and birds building nests.

The envious man left his home.

He walked a long distance, walked over many meadows covered in green leaves, and finally found a small, dry place, looked back at the road he had travelled, and stood still. He stood still and let his roots sink into the ground. He coated himself with green leaves and olives.

The man who washed off his envy still stands there today. He stands still and rustles.

12. THE STORY OF A LONG-LIVED MAN

There was a man. A thief in the night stole the following day from him.

The man grieved, since the following day took with it the following day's sunrise, the following day's high noon, the following day's peaceful evening, and the following day's night, adorned by the full moon and the sparkling stars.

The following day took with it the following day's hope, wondering about the following day, today's memory arising tomorrow, and all joy and sweetness about the days gone by.

With the following day disappeared the future days belonging to it.

The man was left with only today's day.

Early in the morning, the man got up out of his bed, looked at his family, all still slumbering sweetly, lit today's candle and left his home.

Today's sun was rising, the man's last sunrise ...

And the man took off into the day.

He gave the dog a pat.

He sent the livestock away with the village herd.

He took a walk around the yard, fixed the broken fence, and heightened the short end.

He trimmed the vineyard.

He rid the tree of its dry branches.

He gave his eldest son some work to do.

He scolded the middle child.

He made some affectionate noises at the youngest.

He avoided his wife's eyes.

He called over to his neighbor. His neighbor called over back to him.

He dug the ground. He hacked the soil. He crossbred the plants. He sowed the seeds. He reaped the harvest. He buried what was to bury. He gave away what was to give.

He settled the debt.

Afternoon arrived.

The man rested under the tree's shade.

He remembered what was to be remembered. He forgot what was to be forgotten. He redeemed what was to be redeemed. Joy brought him joyfulness. Sadness made him sad. Fear frightened him. The cold made him feel cold. Warmth warmed him up.

For a second it struck him that tomorrow's day was

not to come, and melancholy pushed upon him.

Instantly he rose and straightened up.

Then:

He praised his eldest son.

He gave his middle child some work to do.

He made some affectionate noises at the youngest.

He caressed his wife.

He chopped wood for the winter.

Evening was setting.

The dog started barking.

The village's herd was returning home ...

An exhausted, hungry, thirsty traveler with an instrument came up to his house.

He bid him inside. He hosted his guest. He lit him the fireplace. He let him bathe. He fed him bread. He gave him wine.

They hummed together. They sang together.

The guest rose up. He wished to leave.

The whole family poured onto the balcony to wave the guest goodbye ...

Today's sun hadn't yet set.

Rain arrived, and rain went, and the rainbow adorned the sky.

Late noon arrived, with its cooling shades and vital breeze, which was to remain.

Peaceful evening settled, and the blackbird was singing.

Full moon arose, and the stars were sparkling.

The traveler with his instrument was following his road to the west ...

Today's candle had not yet died away.

13. THE STORY OF A MAN WHO TRADED WELL

A man once lived in our village. Some time ago, the man owned a small house and garden with a fence around it. In his grassy garden stood a cozy little hut. Behind the hut there was a vineyard and a fruit garden. In one corner of the garden was a well that always had cold and crystal-clear water. Many birds and animals sprang around in his garden and a single big, fluffy dog guarded the house faithfully.

In the mornings, once the first rays of the sun were falling onto the garden, the man would set to work and would labor until late into the evening. Only in the evenings would the tired and worn-out man sit himself comfortably by the fireplace with his children and wife, tune the chonguri-guitar, and sing sweetly and harmoniously together with them. Nighttimes, when everyone else would be peacefully asleep, the man would talk with the far-away stars. Nearby, a blackbird would sing. To put it in a sentence, our man's house and garden was more than he could ask for.

However, one day his luck turned on him. The man sold all of his property. He sold the vineyard and the fruit garden. He sold the well's cold and crystal-clear water, and the vivid grass in front of the hut where the birds and pet animals had been moving around. He sold his loyal dog. He sold the garden's night sky with its talking stars. He also sold the singing blackbirds.

On the other hand, with the sum he gained, he purchased half of the village, but what was incredible was that his property was included as well. We all condemned the man, but in our hearts we were envious of him and if we had had the opportunity, we too would have sold our properties without hesitation.

There is one more thing to say ... Because he had sold them, until his death, the man didn't once visit his ancestral house and garden. He also never again looked up at the sky to talk to the stars.

14. THE STORY OF A DREAMY MAN

There was once a man, a hopeless dreamer.

He was the head of a full household. Since creating a family, the fire in his fireplace never died out. He had a virtuous and beautiful wife, and seven children. He was hospitable, pitiful and soft-hearted.

You wouldn't find anyone in the village hurt by him.

He wept with the weeping and rejoiced with the joyful.

He was very hard-working.

He ate only what he had harvested.

He loved everyone, and everyone loved him: humans and livestock, vines and fruits, oaks and clovers, rain and wind, crystal-clear springs and moldy boulders, dusk and dawn.

He also had a black-and-white cat, but he couldn't figure out whether the cat was black with white spots, or white with black spots.

Before going to sleep, the dreamy man would go around the house and listen to his peacefully sleeping family's breathing, then would head to his bed and climb into it, the black and white cat would curl up by his feet and fall asleep, and only he himself would put his hands behind his head, gaze up at the ceiling and would fall into deep wondering: If only I were alone, kithless, not loving anybody, and nobody loving me, not worrying for anyone's worries, and not being happy for anyone's happiness, having a heart of stone, having no principle, be sinful and joyful for being so. If only I were revengeful and not forgiving of anyone. If only everyone feared me and was in awe of me.

While wondering wistfully he as well would fall asleep.

His life proceeded in this fashion; only his dreams never came true.

15. THE STORY OF A MAN WHO LOST HIS SELF

There was once a man; he lost his self.

Dawn came, and the man woke up. From the morning on, emptiness followed him. The man couldn't even get anything from his dreams, except fear and despair. He had a flavorless breakfast and right away he started searching, only he didn't know what he was searching for.

He searched in the dark and bright corners of the room.

He searched in the closet with the smudgy mirror, between new and old clothes, he searched in the wall cupboard, between washed and unwashed sheets, he searched in the pile of dust under the bed, he searched on the bookshelves, in books and in between books, he searched between items on his desk, he searched in the drawers, in between yellow papers with notes written on them and with their corners nibbled by mice, in between old, tied bundles of letters …

His memories started to move around, and now he began to search in between them for what he had lost, but the thing he searched for remained beyond his memories …

He became thirsty and drank some water.

Maybe he lost it in the woman's comfort, or in betrayal, or maybe even in his loyalty. Maybe in the wind or in the rain. Maybe he lost it in the moonlit night, whatever he was searching for, or in between the stars. Maybe he lost what he was searching for in the rising sun, or in the colors of the sunset.

Sounds and songs started playing inside of him and now he searched in between these. Landscapes replaced landscapes, the river's thicketed banks, the meadow's poppy army, uninhabited areas, waterless areas, dry ground, grassy meadows, cold, misty mountains, and stormy and calm seas.

There were known and unknown faces: worrying, smiling, thoughtful, direct and indirect, living and dead.

He lay down. He tried to go to sleep. Sleep didn't touch him. He closed his eyes and locked up his body. He walked around inside of himself as if around an abandoned house. He was searching for something, but he didn't know what. Maybe he was searching for pain. To his dismay nothing hurt him.

The evening arrived. A breeze softly fluttered the thin, transparent curtain. The man moved an armchair to the window and fell into deep thought. He then looked at his hands and they seemed foreign to him.

It was then that he realized that he had lost his self.

He sat for a while in the armchair.

Then he got up and left the house.

He firmly closed the door.

The man searched for his self the whole evening, the whole night. He searched in streets he recognized and streets he didn't recognize. On deserted shores. On blazing, crowded squares. Everyone was walking silently and aimlessly all over the place. One could only hear their footsteps.

The man followed the crowd.

He found himself in a wild garden. Here and there, in between leaves, the buzzing lights above him barely shone down on him. In the garden many people were also searching for their lost selves, and in between these were also people who had already been abandoned by their selves. They searched each other blindly, crying out desperately, sighing and moaning.

One by one the people disappeared, souls emptied and, turning to shadows, they joined the darkness.

The garden became empty and the leaves rustled on.

The man also came out of the garden with a large, white dog following him like a shadow.

The man was returning home.

The dog followed the man all the way to his house. If the man would stop, the dog immediately stopped somewhere behind him as well.

As soon as he arrived at his front door he looked around, but the dog was out of sight.

He found his door slightly open.

He entered the room and turned on the light.

In the armchair by the window there sat a stranger.

He glanced at who had come in and turned back to gaze at his hands. A breeze softly fluttered the thin, transparent curtain.

The man realized that he was not himself. On his spot there stood an old closet with a smudgy mirror.

Dawn was coming.

16. THE STORY OF A MAN WHO HANDED HIS WILL OVER TO THE WIND

There was once a man who handed his will over to the wind.

The wind snatched it up like a feather and showed the ground to the will.

The wind made the will, being in a state of pleasure, heavy like hail, and smashed it against the ground.

At the bottom the will met a stone.

Sometimes the wind forged the will in fire; sometimes he gave it to the water. Sometimes he led it across a narrow bridge, and sometimes he put obstacles in front of it on a wide road.

Sometimes he delighted it with an encounter; sometimes he saddened it with a separation.

He mixed it in the rubbish that had been left by everyone.

He made it taste the sourness of injustice; he filled it with the sweetness of justice.

He frightened it with fear; he calmed it with calmness.

He indebted it with its dreams, he made it settle its

debts through daily labor.

He led it to sin, then calmed its soul with tears of regret and showed it purity.

He made it loath greed through wealth; he made it love generosity through poverty.

He dressed the desperately frozen will with hope and warmed it.

He cured with love its blisters of evil temptations.

Fallen through faithlessness, he revived it with faith.

In the end, during a drought, he turned it into a cloud and made it rain.

17. THE STORY OF A MAN WHO LOVED LIFE

He was home. He loved being at home. He was outside. He loved being outside.

He loved being alone and he loved being amongst others.

He was joyful. He loved being in joy. He was sorrowful. He loved being in sorrow.

He loved worrying and he loved being worriless.

He stood in the rain. He loved being in the rain. He stood in the sun. He loved being in the sun.

He also loved the shadow ...

He loved the moonlit nights and he loved the moonless nights.

He also loved the stars ...

He had work. He loved being at work. He was without work. He loved being without work.

He loved mountains and he loved valleys.

He also loved forests ...

He also loved wheat fields ...
He also loved cliffs and he also loved the mist.
He also loved the wind and he also loved storms.
He also loved the breeze ...
He also loved the rustling of leaves.
He also loved the river and he also loved woods.
He also loved the sea and he also loved springs.
He also loved moldy boulders.
He also loved violets ...
He also loved roses ...
He also loved snowflakes ...
He also loved daisies ...
He loved blackbirds and he also loved nightingales.
He was free and he loved freedom.
He was captured and he learnt to love captivity.
He also loved waterfalls ...
He also loved rainbows ...
He was here and he loved life.
He went there and he welcomed death.
... on his tombstone it read: here lies a man, he
loved life.

18. THE STORY OF A MAN WHO MADE HIMSELF MASTER

There was once a lazy man; he was too lazy to do
anything.

He was too lazy to wake up and too lazy to go to
sleep.

When he was hungry, he was too lazy to eat. When
he was thirsty, he was too lazy to drink. He was too

lazy to go right and too lazy to go left. When he was at home, he was too lazy to be at home; when he was outside, he was too lazy to be outside.

He was too lazy to say anything and too lazy to stay silent.

He was too lazy to hammer in the nail and he was too lazy to pull out the nail.

Finally he became too lazy of being lazy and became master of himself.

From this day on, the man couldn't get a rest from himself from morning till midnight.

Not budging from his spot and legs crossed, he sat deeply in an armchair, puffed away on his hookah, and forged himself new orders.

19. THE STORY OF A MAN WHO DIDN'T GET TO KNOW HIMSELF

There was a man; he didn't get to know himself . . .

When the man went to sleep, he himself woke up.

When the man woke up, he himself stood up.

When the man stood up, he himself sat.

When the man sat, he himself left.

When the man left, he himself arrived.

Then:

When he cried, the man laughed.

When he listened to silence, the man sang.

When he sought light, the man struggled in darkness.

When he told himself the truth, the man lied to himself.

When he felt regret, the man made a heart of
stone ...

And again:

When he was at home, all alone, the man roamed
with crowds of people.

When he started on a long journey, the man
strolled around close by.

In the end, the man died. He himself stood above
the departed and gazed upon him but didn't recognize
himself, although he had seen his face somewhere.

20. THE STORY OF A MAN ON WHOSE SPOT EMPTINESS WAS LEFT

There was a man, a lover of wealth.

He collected everything: gold and silver, pearls
and incredibly valuable crystal dishes; the finest
furniture ...

He built beautiful palaces, stunning gardens of all
sorts, pools, and fountains ...

He built a high wall around his residence and lived
in pleasure and extreme luxury until his death.

But when he felt that death was near, he realized
that he didn't want to part with his earthly
possessions, and therefore hung everything he had
upon his soul and had everything buried with him.

It turned out that no one needed his treasures in
the next world; in this one, though, he left a big
empty spot.

21. THE STORY OF A MAN WHOM EVERYONE THOUGHT DIDN'T EXIST

There was a man who was to himself; and everyone thought he wasn't there ...

There was the sky and earth, there was brightness and darkness, there was the sun and the moon, there were stars ...

And there was a man who was to himself ...

There was dusk and dawn, there was north and south, there was east and west, there was the second and the century, there was near and far, there was right and left ...

And there was a man whom everyone thought didn't exist, since he was to himself ...

There was love and hate, there was loyalty and betrayal, there was hope and despair, there was sourness and sweetness, there was peace and anxiety ...

And there was a man who was to himself, and everyone thought he didn't exist ...

There was justice and injustice, there was ruthlessness and mercy, there was the murdered and the murderer, there was fullness and also emptiness ...

And all of us were right here ...

And there was a man who was to himself, and everything and each thing went through him, and his due place was held by the murdered and murderer, offended and offender, north and east, brightness and darkness, far and near, law and lawlessness, the sun, the moon, and the stars ...

They would come in and find each other, debate and reconcile ... And would calm down ...

And, finally, death entered him and he obtained his due place ...

It was his alone ...

GEORGIAN LITERATURE SERIES

The Georgian Literature Series aims to bring to an English-speaking audience the best of contemporary Georgian fiction. Made possible thanks to the financial support of the Georgian National Book Centre and the Ministry of Culture and Monument Protection of Georgia, the Series began with four titles, officially published in January 2014. Available in January 2015 are four new titles, offering readers a choice of Georgian literary works.

www.dalkeyarchive.com

GEORGIAN LITERATURE SERIES

Erlom Akhvlediani
Vano and Niko & other stories / Translated by Mikheil Kakabadze
Akhvlediani's minimalist prose pieces are Kafkaesque parables presenting individual experience as a quest for the other. ISBN 978-1-62897-106-4 / $15.95 US

Lasha Bugadze
The Literature Express / Translated by Maya Kiasashvili
The Literature Express is a riotous parable about the state of literary culture, the European Union, and our own petty ambitions—be they professional or amorous. ISBN 978-1-56478-726-2 / $16.00 US

Zaza Burchuladze
adibas / Translated by Guram Sanikidze
A "war novel" without a single battle scene, Zaza Burchuladze's English-language debut anatomizes the Western world's ongoing "feast in the time of plague." ISBN 978-1-56478-925-9 / $15.50 US

Tamaz Chiladze
The Brueghel Moon / Translated by Maya Kiasashvili
The novel of the famous Georgian writer, poet and playwright Tamaz Chiladze focuses on moral problems / issues, arisen as a result of the too great self-assuredness of psychologists. ISBN 978-1-62897-093-7 / $14.95 US

Mikheil Javakhishvili
Kvachi / Translated by Donald Rayfield
This is, in brief, the story of a swindler, a Georgian Felix Krull, or perhaps a cynical Don Quixote, named Kvachi Kvachantiradze: womanizer, cheat, perpetrator of insurance fraud, bank-robber, associate of Rasputin, filmmaker, revolutionary, and pimp. ISBN 978-1-56478-879-5 / $17.95 US

Zurab Karumidze
Dagny
Fact and fantasy collide in this visionary, literary "feast" starring historical Norwegian poet and dramatist Dagny Juel (1867-1901), a beautiful woman whose life found her falling victim to one deranged male fantasy after another. ISBN 978-1-56478-928-0 / $15.00 US

Anna Kordzaia-Samadashvili
Me, Margarita / Translated by Victoria Field & Natalia Bukia-Peters
Short stories about men and women, love and hate, sex and disappointment, cynicism and hope—perhaps unique in that none of the stories reveal the time or place in they occur: the world is too small now for it to matter. ISBN 978-1-56478-875-7 / $15.95 US

Aka Morchiladze
Journey to Karabakh / Translated by Elizabeth Heighway
One of the best-selling novels ever released in Georgia, and the basis for two feature films, this is a book about the tricky business of finding—and defining—liberty. ISBN 978-1-56478-928-0 / $15.00 US

www.dalkeyarchive.com